CW00972056

How To Seduce A Woman

The Secrets That Women Don't Want You To Know

Ricardo Del Monte

CONTENTS

Published by Honey Farm Books
www.honeyfarmbooks.com

1. INTRODUCTION

About Me

Hi.

My name is Ricardo. Ricardo Del Monte.

I'm 35 years old. I'm dashingly handsome, extraordinarily funny, single and when fully erect, my penis measures 8.2 inches.

I rise at 6am every morning and spend an hour in the heated pool that sits underneath my executive apartment block. I wear blue speedos to show off my Adonis-like physique. After that, I sit on my balcony, eat freshly sliced grapefruit and sip Hacienda La Esmeralda coffee. The view from my balcony extends over Cardiff Bay. On sunny days, I watch the small boats chugging across the bay. My apartment has two bedrooms. One for me, one for my House of Fraser suits. My apartment is carpeted throughout with heavy-pile carpet.

In my garage sits my BMW 6 Series. Its powerful V8 engine, with its high-precision direct injection and twin-turbo accelerates with an outstanding 450hp. It's white in colour and has leather seats. I never use air fresheners as I prefer the aroma of the warm leather. I never turn the radio on either as I prefer to listen to the sound of the purring V8.

I work at Bissman Financial Services. We're located in Bissman House. It's one of those tall, posh buildings you see down Cardiff Bay. I'm one of the directors of the company. I've worked my way up through the office. More importantly, I've had fun getting there. Oh. And by fun, yes, I mean that I've slept my way to the top.

Call me a male slut if you like, but that's a title I'm rather smug about. It's nothing to be ashamed of. One day, I'll be an old man. In the meantime, I'm helping myself to whoever I like. And there's no stopping me.

That's right. I can have any woman I want. I can seduce any one of them. When a new girl starts at the office, I know that they owe me one. Why? Because I've hired them. And I can fire them once I've finished with them too. I hire the good-looking girls with the big tits. And when they strut into the office in their high heels on their first day, I'm mentally undressing them. More than that, I'll be planning my way to undress them for real and to get them into bed. It doesn't matter if they're single, engaged or married - they're all fair game in my world.

You see, I'm what you call 'a player', and a damn good one at that. I eat pussy for breakfast, dinner and tea. Sometimes, I even have it for supper. I love it. I can't get enough. And guess what? I don't have to pay for it or beg for it. I'm the man who makes husbands jealous. The other lads in the office are in awe of me. They consider me a legend. I am God.

Except none of this is true. Well, not the first bit anyway. My name's not Ricardo Del Monte (you seriously thought my name was Ricardo Del Monte?) It's Richard. Richard Evans. Hi.

I'm from a small town called Barry in South Wales. I drive a Fiat Panda Dynamique and I have Coco Pops for breakfast and supper (as long as my nan's remembered to get some when she goes to

Iceland).

But one thing is true – I do work in an office. I work in a call centre. I've been here seven months now. I'm the guy who tells you the times of the trains. We've probably spoken on several occasions.

And another thing is true. I've slept with a number of the girls here in the office in the short time that I've been here. And not just the ugly ones. I consider myself the call centre lothario. No-one else in this office has gotten as many girls into bed as I have. Apart from Tony. He's my main rival at the moment. He has a big wide face and poppy-out eyes like he's forever had a cucumber stuck up his arsehole. He's always happy. The girls love him because he's so lovely (awww). I don't dislike the guy - in fact, I like the competition. But I'm determined not to let him take the title of King of the Office.

The girls I've had weren't just all the office slags either – these were proper tidy girls (between me and you, I did do Sharon 'Turbo Tits' Williams, the ugliest girl in the entire office. But that was just a 'pity shag' and I don't include her on my list - not unless I'm trying to outdo Tony and his list).

So what's the first lesson you've learnt from this book already?

That's right:

Trust no-one.

I lied to you. Ok, so I don't share my surname with a brand of tinned fruit products. And I don't have a BMW 6 Series. But, trust me, your well-spent couple of quid on this book will not be going to waste.

There is one thing I am going to show you -

and that's how to bed any woman you want.

Yes, ANY woman.

And I'm going to share my secret with you. Why? Well you've taken the trouble of buying my book firstly. I appreciate that. There's a lot of other books out there that offer the same sort of thing. And I know you probably only picked this one because it was one of the cheapest ones you came across. But I don't hold that against you. In fact, I applaud you. Times are hard. But believe me, I can show you how to bag a top lay.

Secondly, I'm going to share my secret with you because I think it'll bring about world peace. It's not inconceivable but that's all I can think of right now.

And thirdly, I just want to show off about the girls I've had.

How to Use This Book

Ok, so we've established that you've bought this book as you'd like to learn how to seduce women. Correct?

'But I'm a pretty average guy.' I hear you say. Well whoopy-fucking-do. Aren't we all?

The fact is, that you don't need a BMW 6 Series to get a girl into bed. Sure, you can take her to Asda in it but it's not going to take her to heaven and back (not unless you accidentally reverse over her in it). No – it's you, your mind, your personality, your confidence and a few little tricks that's going to bag you a top-notch intercourse session with a tidy bird.

Firstly, some rules:

• If you want to get a woman into bed, there should be no trickery, deception or coercion. Your lady should be willing, conscious and should open her legs voluntarily. Fortunately, you've got me, call centre lothario and master of seduction here to show you how.

• No getting someone into bed just to win a bet. That just ain't right. Have some respect will you?

The first thing you need to understand is that women are not like us lads. For a start, they've got titties and a big hairy minge. Not only that, but they think differently to us. Think back to 10,000 B.C. (10,000 years before Coronation Street) when men and women simply grunted at each other (this still happens in some areas of Wales, I'm told). Men were the hunter/gatherers and the women were the home (cave) makers.

After the lads had come back from a hard day of hunting woolly mammoths and sabre-toothed tigers, they'd need some way of letting their unruly and unkempt hair down. To do this, they'd expect a spot of 'corrective training' from their cavelady, who had mostly been sat around doing nothing all day apart from swatting flies and picking their own toenails.

Of course, if the lads did get lucky, they could have their few minutes of fun before heading down to the prehistoric pub for some mead or whatever it was that they drank back then.
The caveladies however, could potentially become pregnant after this. Over time, these caveladies became fussy about who they opened their hairy legs to, not wanting to become saddled with a nine month pregnancy for any old saddo caveman.

So cavemen started trying to impress these ladies to give themselves a better chance of getting laid with them. They'd bring back bigger and more expensive cuts of dinosaurs to put in the fridge. Some took to drawing hunting scenes on the inside of caves to impress the girls but these lads were often considered 'arty farty types' and were often overlooked for their more 'manly' counterparts.
As the years went on, it became tradition for ladies to mate with the cavemen who brought back the biggest and juiciest slabs of dinosaur meat, today's equivalent of a pay packet. They were also drawn to the lads who drove the flashiest Fred Flintstone cars (you know the ones with the feet poking out the bottom).

A few of the 'average' cavemen lads noticed this behaviour. They wanted cave pussy but didn't have the means to go out clubbing dinosaurs over the head and dragging them back to the cave. They weren't gifted with big muscles or top of the range Fred Flintstone cars. So they got a bit sneaky about it all. And it worked a treat.

So what did they do? They set about inventing fly swatters and toe nail clippers. While the hairy guys were out fist-fighting big dinosaurs, these sneaky lads stayed at home. They visited the ladies who were sitting around all day swatting flies and picking their own toenails. These lads presented these ladies with their new-fangled inventions. They spent time with these ladies, talking to them about their day-to-day problems (essentially flies and long toe nails) and building a thing called trust. I'll come on to that later in the book, but don't forget these lads – they were pioneers because it wasn't long before the ladies started developing feelings for them. And while the hunter cavemen were out doing battle with mythical creatures and chopping them up to bring home, these sneaky lads were already at home banging their wives. Christ, they'd even get invited back over for tea by the hunters themselves when they got back as way of saying 'thank you' for keeping their wives happy with their fly swatters and toe nail clippers. If only they knew.

Lazy but clever see?

Now you may assume that from the title of this book that your seductee will have no choice in this matter of being seduced. That they will be somehow unaware that they are actually being seduced.

Wrong, wrong, wrong.

The purpose of this book is to get someone to fancy you, and at their behest, willingly clamber into bed with you. You'll be playing by all the rules, not upsetting anyone (maybe a few boyfriends or husbands but we'll deal with that later eh?) and still keeping them as a Facebook friend afterwards. Seduction is all about persuading someone that you are irresistible and that they want you as much as you want them. They'll be gagging for you.

Imagine for a moment, David Attenborough doing a documentary about leopards. In this particular episode, there's a close up of a leopard, in a tree, eyes scouring the plains of wherever they live (I really can't be arsed to Google it sorry).

You need to picture yourself as that leopard. Choosing its winnings. Eyeing its prey.

That's you. And that woman who was in your mind when you first thought about buying this book is about to willingly become yours. For a short time anyway. But hey, that's all you need, right?

At the moment, you are this leopard I just mentioned, lying in the shade at rest, probably licking your spotty bollocks or something. But you're hungry.

Just then a herd of gnus stroll past. Gnu - it's a type of wildebeest. (Once upon a time, there was a Daddy Gnu, a Mummy Gnu and a Baby Gnu. One day, they all went for a walk and they all fell off a cliff and died. And that was the end of the gnus. And now for the weather forecast).

Your eyes scan the great herds of gnus. There are some skanky-looking ones of course. But there are some lovely looking ones too. Which one are you going to have? The easy skanky-looking ones that can't even be arsed to grunt with the rest of them?

Or the tasty-looking one?

You lick your lips in anticipation.

You get up, descend the tree and stretch your legs.

Yes, my friend. It's time to hunt.

2. BACKGROUND SKILLS

Perceived Confidence

Imagine now for a moment that you're sat on a jet plane that's just taken off from Cardiff airport. The plane is climbing high into the sky. You've ordered a Babycham from the air hostess and now you're annoying the person behind you by reclining your seat and getting comfy with a copy of Bella (or something similar).

The Captain comes on the tannoy and announces himself. He says his name is Derek. This is what he announces:

"Good morning. My name's Derek and I'm your captain for the day. As you may have noticed, we've just taken off from the airport and are flying through the air at some 500mph. We've got some heavy weather ahead of us. Fingers crossed, I'm hoping that we're going to be ok, especially since this is my first time flying this plane and I'm not very good at landing. I'm not sure at what time we're likely to be landing either but if you look out of the window and you see the ground, we probably will have landed somehow. Thank you."

Anus twitching? Babycham suddenly gone flat?

Hm. You see, confidence is everything.

Here's Tim, our other pilot.

"Good morning. My name's Tim and I'm your captain for the day. As you may have noticed, we've just taken off from the airport and are flying through the air at some 500mph. We've got some heavy weather ahead of us but I can assure you that you're going to be in safe hands. I've flown this type of plane a thousand times before and I'll make sure that we get you to your destination on time and in one piece. So sit back, enjoy your Babycham and your latest issue of Bella. There's a great feature on page 17 about a 40-stone man who found a rusty bicycle up the crack of his arse. Laters dudes."

Right. So who would you rather be flying with? Capt. Derek or Capt. Tim?

That's right. Capt. Tim. He's going to get us there safe and sound. And if even if he doesn't; even if he takes us straight into the side of a mountain ('Ladies and Gentleman, we are just putting down here in the side of this mountain. Thank you for flying SleazyJet'), he's made us feel that we can trust him.

It's how he's made us **feel**.

It's the same when it comes to seducing a woman. It's how you make her **feel**. She may **feel** fat and ugly. She may well **be** fat and ugly. But you've got to make her **feel** like she's a million dollars. Why? Because she's more likely to come back to you for more. The more she comes back, the more secure she'll feel with you. She's unlikely to remember **everything** you say - but she'll sure to hell remember how you made her **feel** (end of over-the-top bold font usage. Sorry).

Let's think for a minute as to why women are drawn to the baddies in movies. Well, these baddies have a plan, and they know how to go about fulfilling it. Alright, so you get some smart-arsed goodie coming along and saving the day but he's only reacting to something that the baddy has done. The baddie is the one leading the way, taking things forward. The baddy is setting himself up for a fall but he has a vision, an ideology – and the motivation to implement it. He has the conviction, the confidence. Ever seen a dithering baddie who's lacking in confidence? No. And the poncey goodies are the weak, flawed ones who somehow, by a stroke of luck, win the day.

Now before you head down the local fancy dress shop for a Darth Vader costume, I'm not asking you to be a bad person. I'm asking you to be confident.

'But Rich, I'm not a confident person.' I hear you say.

Well Tim wasn't either. In fact, like Derek, he'd never flown a plane like that before. In fact, he'd never flown a plane before. Not ever. But we chose him because he was apparently confident. He made us feel that we could relax and read our latest issue of Bella magazine with a Babycham.

But Tim **feigned** his confidence.

Oh the scamp! How could he?

Well, believe it or not, it's what a lot of people do. Those big-mouthed celebrities on the telly - they're all full of themselves. But inside, they're all eaten up, riddled with insecurities and knotted with anxiety.

So if you're not confident, pretend to be. It'll do two things – make you look more confident (and therefore more attractive). Secondly, you'll get into the habit of doing things confidently. As a result, you will become more confident. And therefore more attractive. And therefore more confident (and so on). You get the idea.

This is your first step towards seducing a lady. Practice it. By the end of this book, that girl's ovaries will be crying out for you.

By the way, here are a few things that kill confidence:

• Comparing yourself to others. You could spend your entire life doing this. And what do you do? You compare your weaknesses to their strengths. You're never going to win. You see their 'showreel' and look at what you don't have. You have strengths, like they have weaknesses. Ok, so Dave down the end of the office has a flash car, a penthouse, more money in the bank than he cares for. And his knob is probably twice the size of yours. But think about what you have that he doesn't. Go on. Think about it….go on, I'll wait here…what about that lovely Stella Artois chalice you nicked from The Three Horseshoes last month? Bet he hasn't got one of them has he? No. I bet he has to drink his Skol straight out of the can like a commoner. So there – you have something he doesn't have (better examples are available on request).

• Criticism is not the bad thing that you think it is. People are just kindly pointing out ways for you to improve and become a better person. That's unless they're telling you that your gut's too big or that you smell of piss. But even then, a male corset and a quick wash will make you look and smell ten times better than you did before. They were just being kind by pointing out these defects. They were doing you a favour. Listen to them.

• Rejection is another confidence killer. Sure, take some time out of your life to process the rejection. But don't go spending weeks wallowing in self-pity though eh? The earlier you accept the rejection and attempt to move on from it, the easier a time you're going to have. Remember that the rejection says nothing about you as a person.

Getting rejected is part of life and it is not a personal attack. That's unless they are point-blank refusing to sleep with you because you look like Russell Grant after an all-dayer.

3. OPENING PREPARATION

Where do we start with the seduction process?

I'll tell you now – **we start at the end**.

'What? Are you bonkers? Have you gone totally mad?' I hear you cry.

Trust me my friend. Achieving any goal involves just that – setting a goal. If you head up the field with your mates to have a kick around with a football, what do you do if you find that the Council have taken down all the goals because it's the end of the season? That's right – you set up your own goal with a few jumpers and that plastic bag full of beer.

Let's suppose you've parked up your Ford Mondeo Ghia at Cardiff City Stadium to see the place where the Premiership sides used to play. And let's suppose that you want to have lunch at the Plough and Harrow in Monknash, Glamorgan, some 20 miles away. Let's say that you've never been there before. Maybe you have. But let's pretend that you haven't – please stick with it for the purpose of this analogy. And let's pretend that you have a car – a nice shiny Ford Mondeo Ghia.

How do you get there?

Obviously, you get on A4232, follow it to the M4. Join the M4 heading west. Take the A473 exit from the M4 towards Bridgend/Pencoed/Pen-y-bont. At the roundabout, take the first exit onto A473, going through two roundabouts and at the third roundabout, take the 2nd exit onto Bypass Rd/A48. Go through another roundabout and after about a mile, take the first exit onto Ewenny Rd/

B4265. Continue to follow the B4265, and after about four miles, turn right onto Heol Las. Just under two miles, you'll find the Plough and Harrow there on the right.

So what if you don't know all that?

That's right – **you plan**.

You get that old crinkly map out from the boot of your car (the map that had screen wash tipped all over it back in 1997). Or you use Google maps. Or if you're really lazy, you use Satnav, which does all the planning for you.

Planning for your ultimate goal is imperative. Figuring out what you want (fanny) and how you're going to get there is the surefire way to success. And how do you know that you've reached your destination?

You'll be up to your nuts in guts and patting yourself on the back (though not at the same time hopefully).

This book is guaranteed to change your life forever.

You ready?

Ok. Here's how.

Have a look around your workplace. I'm presuming that you're working at the cutting edge of British industry in a call centre like myself. I'm also guessing that there are a few ladies there that you wouldn't mind poking with your poking stick. Am I right? What about that new girl? What about that girl who works on Floor 2 - the one with the wobbly jugglies? What about your boss? Surely that'd look good on your CV of Love if you nailed her?

The fact is, you can have any one of those girls. Yes, really. You can. Yes, even the ones that seems 'untouchable'.

What you'll need in bucket loads is patience. If a woman tells you to 'piss off you stinking piece of rotting shit', that doesn't necessarily mean that she's not interested in you. It just means that she's having a bad day. Maybe she has PMT. Or maybe she's just playing hard to get. Patience is key, my friend.

Now. What I want you to do is to close your eyes. That's right. Close them.

Actually, open them again because you won't be able to read this next bit.....you there? Hello?

Ok. Welcome back. Before you disappeared, I was waffling on about deciding who you'd like to seduce.

The best way to do this is to compare yourself to your place in the world if you were a football team. Are you a high-flying, successful Premiership side or are you struggling to prop up the Evo-Stick One (Northern) League? This decision will help you decide how much patience you're going to need. Now clearly, if you look and act like Benny off Crossroads, you're going to need a bit more patience than others.

Next, consider in which league your seductee lies. Needless to say, the higher the league compared to you, the bigger the giant-killing FA Cup round will be. But it can be done. Remember that perceived confidence I told you about earlier.

Right, so you've decided on someone. For the sake of argument, let's call her Glinda. Actually no. Let's call her something else. Sounds far too much like something off the Wizard of Oz. Let's called her Angharad instead. Angharad it is.

Angharad's a 28 year-old girl from Caerphilly. She works in telesales and often tops the 'Who'd You Most Like To Shag' lists that do the rounds in the office. She has straight brown hair and porcelain-like skin; she has eyes the colour of swirling dark chocolate, flecked with hazelnut; that deep brown of the winter trees at twilight; the colour of apple pips, mottled like varnished cork.

She has a petite, delicate nose and soft plumptious red lips that you just want to rest your sleepy head on. She sits there, twirling her hair round her Parker pen and leaving lipstick on her paper coffee cup. She's the one you could sit and watch all day. Oh to be her chair for just an hour.

She wears curve-hugging skirts that caress her womanly hips and she always wears a tight white blouse that cups her perfectly-rounded, ample bosoms. If only you could feel the slight pull of the buttons as you slowly undid them. Alas, we're getting ahead of ourselves. Patience!

She's got a Peugeot convertible which she parks in the car park outside the office. The car has a pink fluffy dice hanging from the mirror and a half packet of Love Hearts on the passenger side of the dashboard. At home, she has a small dog called Buster and she has a small tattoo on her right ankle (Angharad, not the dog).

Hell, let's make this a real challenge – yes that's right – her fiancé is a burly marine commando who's away defending the country on a tour of duty. Angharad keeps a photo of him on her work desk. His arms can shift mountains and the gun he holds in his hand could probably take out a tank. They've been together for seven years and are planning on getting married next year in a £30,000 wedding at the Vale Resort.

Angharad is our choice for today. She is going to be the woman of our fantasies for the purpose of this 'project'. When she walks down that aisle next year, she's going to be carrying with her the scandalous secret that you're about to engineer with the techniques that I'm about to show you.

Firstly, you need to make a good impression. So how do you make a good impression?

Surprisingly, it doesn't have to be anything spectacular. You certainly don't need to come in on a zip wire, dressed as Tarzan, singing 'Zippity Doo Dah' or anything daft like that. The key is just to firstly let Angharad know that you exist – and that you're a nice person. A simple 'hi' or 'hello' is sufficient enough to let her know that you work in the same office and to break the ice.

After this, and when you're next on break, just say hello to her. Has a packet of Quavers failed to clear the lip in the vending machine? Is it left hanging there in mid-air, even though the machine has swallowed your 50p piece? Is Angharad waiting to buy herself a Twix? Get into a conversation about how these machines are always getting your Quavers stuck. Tell her about the time when you tried rocking the machine and it set off the alarm. Laugh about it. Share that hilarious story with her. Make her smile. That's all you're aiming for in this initial encounter.

Nothing more, nothing less.

You don't need to go introducing yourself at this stage either. You don't need to ask her any questions. You just need to make her smile.

Got that?

Good.

Let's look at a few other things you need to consider when making this all-important first impression:

• Looking good (or as best as you can) is vital if you're wanting to get Angharad into bed. Unless she's some kind of freak, she, like most women, is going to appreciate a well-groomed, well-kept man. If you've got long hair, unless you look like Viggo Mortensen, do something with it. Certainly don't flick it back off your face at the same time as flicking your head back. Not unless you're wanting to bed a Whitesnake fan (it has been done).

• Despite some women falling for some right examples of pondlife, the majority of women like a clean-looking, smartly-dressed man. Of course, working in a call centre means that for most of the week, you're going to be looking like a young executive in a shirt and tie anyway. But when it comes to Dress-Down Friday, this is where you can really go to town and look smart but casual. A bit like Phil Spencer from Location, Location, Location. My nan loves him. Says she'd love to 'take him to an abandoned house and bang the twat to kingdom come'. If Nan says that, smart is the way to go. Stay away from flip-flops, especially if your toe nails are yellow and gnarled. This also contravenes Health and Safety in the office place as in the event of a fire, you could be the one looking like the daft twat who wears flip-flops.

• Smelling good is important. A splash of Brut or Hai Karate should do the trick but don't go overboard with the Lynx, especially if you haven't washed the last lot off from yesterday. What tends to happen is that you build up a few layers of Lynx which can be overbearing, especially the ones from their Apollo range.

• Later on, if you're out in a club and you're

in with an early chance with your seductee, it's vital that your old boy is clean. Swilling it in a nightclub sink is usually a short-fix solution although the dude selling you aftershave might not want to watch or shake your hand afterwards.

So we've established that you need to be looking your best when you make that initial contact. Where do you go from here?

Well, what you're looking to do from hereon in is essentially build up a friendship, first and foremost.

It all goes back to this trust thing I keep telling you about – trust. A woman will not sleep with someone she doesn't trust (not unless she's been on the Jagermeisters anyway).

Bit, by bit, you can gradually talk to them and get to know them. This is a very important stage in your seduction - it forms the basis for everything else that follows.

Preparing an Exit Strategy

Before you do anything drastic, you need to consider your exit strategy.

An exit strategy is your way of retreating from the seduction process at any time, should anything go wrong. You use this to protect yourself. It's your parachute to safety, your lifeboat should you need to abandon ship mid-Atlantic.

At every stage of the seduction process that I'll be describing over the next few chapters, consider how you can explain away the situation should someone find out that shouldn't eg. jealous boyfriends/husbands.

As part of your exit strategy, you should

consider leaving no compromising trail. In other words, there should be nothing that anyone can come across that will implicate you in any wrong-doing. Ideally, all communication should be deleted permanently, and any incriminating evidence banished for good. Consider yourself a communications ninja.

4. OPENING MOVES

Building a Friendship

The aim of your opening moves is to create a friendship, make her feel that she can trust you and make her feel special.

You'll need to initiate conversation with them. And when you do, talk about **them**. Ask **them** questions. To get in her knickers, you have to get into her mind. Think like a woman. Ask her about the things you really normally wouldn't ask your mates about eg. 'How did you find last night's episode of Masterchef?' or 'Do you think Greg off Masterchef was a little bit too harsh on that poor Chinese lad last night?' Something like that – it doesn't necessarily need to be a Masterchef-based question. Don't go asking her about horses or make-up though. Not unless she's got a particular interest in that area.

What you DON'T want to do is get carried away at this stage. Patience, patience, patience. All good things come to those who wait. Obviously, you'll keep the end game in mind but at this stage of the game, you don't want to let on that you're wanting to give her a jolly good thundering. Not yet, anyway. Remember what I told you - patience.

Flattery is something that can get you places but be careful not to jump in too soon with this. People love being complimented but use it sparingly. Certainly don't go flattering her on her looks at this stage – she's probably heard it all before and she'll just think that you're only after her beaver (which you are but you don't want her to know that). Think of it as if you were writing a letter to your favourite Hollywood actress. She's going to get shitloads of fan mail every day. They're all going to be saying the same thing eg. 'You're beautiful/marry me' etc. You're going to want your letter to stand out. So compliment her on something she cares about (her work, her love of animals or something similar).

A quick story: I wrote to Anneka Rice once when I was younger. I was a big admirer of her arse on Treasure Hunt and I wanted to pound it with my beaver cleaver. Of course, I didn't want to come across as any other Anneka Rice fan who wanted a piece of her arse. So I wrote her a letter complimenting her on her direction-finding abilities and her great understanding of solving cryptic clues. She sent me a signed photo back.

I was 8 years old.

I'd like to think that had I been 20 years older at that point, that she would have sent me a letter asking me to go round her house and tickle her lettuce. If only she could see me now - a call centre lothario. Alas, it was never to be.

But back to the flattery - don't get carried away. If she's got massive tits, compliment her or her ability to handle a customer complaint or something similar. Be a bit different. Show her that you're not like the rest (even though you are).

Take our lovely girl Angharad. As mentioned, she has an ample bosom that often strains to be released from her tight white blouse.

Sigh.

But we aren't going to compliment her on her jugs. No sireee. We're going to compliment

Angharad on her new haircut.

Her new haircut?

Oh yes! This is a tried-and-tested technique of mine that guarantees results. Check this one out:

Once you're on speaking terms, simply ask her if she's had her hair cut. It's as simple as that!

If she hasn't, you can reply by simply saying: "Oh. It looks different today. I like it." She'll love it. And she'll love you. It's how it makes her **feel**.

If she HAS had it cut, you're onto a winner as most fellas don't even notice when their other half has had their hair cut. You'll instantly have one up on her marine commando fiancé. Ask her where she had it cut, whether it's somewhere she always goes. Hold off from complimenting her on her massive tits, even if this first hair-related compliment does go down well. What you're doing is complimenting her but developing a friendship at the same time.

As you develop conversations, drop in subtle hints that you're interested in her life. Be sure to stick to every day topics throughout the conversation - you don't want to discuss anything sexual at this stage. She may be uncomfortable opening up to you at this point about stuff like that. Instead, here are some tips for developing a style of conversation that'll draw her closer to you subconsciously:

• When you are talking to her, let your eyes stay on hers a little longer than necessary - even during those awkward silences. It all goes back to those primal instincts - a gaze that lingers awakens slightly disturbing feelings, inducing the same 'fight or flight' chemicals that race through our veins when we feel lust. When you must look away, drag your eyes away slowly as if you don't really want to. This is a particularly good technique for us men to use, as women always want to feel that a man is absolutely fascinated by them. Whatever you do though, don't just try out-staring her. It'll freak her out and you're likely to get a reputation for being a creepy pervert.

• As you are chatting, let your eyes do some travelling - but only around her face at first. Let your eyes take a little wander over her face, but concentrate on their eyes. If she seems to be enjoying your visual voyage across her boat race, take small side trips to her neck, shoulders and torso. Don't overdo it or you'll freak her out and you're likely to get a reputation for being a creepy pervert.

• Men are shit at reading body signals so learn how to co-react. Watch how your girl reacts to things and then mirror them, being careful to judge the mood as best you can. Show the same emotions as they show – it's a little psychological trick that works on your quarry's subconscious and helps them feel relaxed about being around you. Whatever you do, don't just copy every action that they do. It'll freak her out and you're likely to get a reputation for being a creepy pervert.

• Smiling is often overlooked but it is a simple and crucial technique. The most effective smile to seduce a woman with is a long, lingering one. Make it appear genuine but don't sit there throughout the entire conversation with a permanent grin on your face like you've got an attack of wind. It'll freak her out and you're likely to get a reputation for being a creepy pervert.

• Avoid talking about yourself too much. People like talking about themselves, not listening to your boring shit. Don't talk about ex-girlfriends either, but if you have to, make sure it's in a positive light. If you go slagging off your last shag, Angharad could feel that you'll be talking about her in the same way in a few months' time should she get involved with you.

• When you feel that your conversation is getting somewhere, and that you have some things in common, don't be afraid to ask questions like "What do you think about that?" Women love to talk about their feelings and their opinions on things. Whereas us lads like to keep things under our hats, it's fine to show a bit of a feminine touch to impress your woman. She'll appreciate it, even if you don't.

• If you're in a group of people, try and introduce a 'private joke' between you and your girl. This not only creates a unique bond between you but it also subconsciously 'pairs you off' from the group.

• Know when to back off. If you're wanting her to come back for more, you're going to need to ration yourself.

• If the conversation dries up, don't just sit there like a twat. Have an 'emergency topic' to talk about – it could be anything – the price of Freddos for instance. Or Space Raiders.

Developing your conversations in the office at this stage is key to the success of your seduction. Back in the good old days, before the internet was really introduced to the workplace, we relied on a thing called a telephone to converse with each other. It was quite a feat of modern engineering – you'd simply pick up what was called a 'receiver' which had two main bits to it – one to speak into and the other to listen to the person on the 'other end of the phone' with. It was essentially a device that converted changes in an electric current into sound but it transformed the way that people spoke to each other. Jokes that were told in Bristol could now be laughed at in Blackpool – simply down to the fact that people in Blackpool could now hear jokes being told in Bristol.

Before the invention of the telephone, people relied on 'writing' to each other. Believe it or not, this involved actually writing words down with a pen and paper, sadly now a long-lost tradition. Some people used to send 'letters' (written handwriting on bits of paper) to each other. These would be posted into special red 'postboxes' – you may still see some historical examples of these dotted around your town and city. They are more commonly used to discard doggy poo bags these days.

Email is another common way of developing your friendship in work too. When email was first invented, us executive lotharios thought all our Christmasses had come at once. In an instant, we were able to contact any woman in the office just by typing in a name. Flirting could be carried out almost unnoticed by anyone else in the office, including our bosses.

Of course, for many years, we were able to get away with sending all kinds of filth to each other by email. Then Facebook came along and bosses got scared. They started snooping around all emails and private messages. By all means, develop your friendship via email. In fact, use a mixture of all these methods (if you are trained in the art of writing) of communication to develop your friendship in conjunction with your verbal exchanges. Just be careful that you don't get caught out. This could jeopardise your mission.

If you feel comfortable, you may want to invest in a small gift. It needn't be expensive – just something small that shows that you've thought about what you've bought. Maybe she's shown an interest in Monster Munch crisps during a break time conversation. Why not buy her a packet on your way into work one morning? You could perhaps, buy her a small teddy bear that she can keep on her desk. Every time she looks at it, she'll think of you.

As they say, it's the little things that mean a lot.

Building Trust

Building trust is vital but as you're doing this, you'll be looking for a valid reason to have contact outside work with her. You can be bold and ask her if she's on Facebook if you want, or you can be pretty sneaky about it (remember those sneaky cavemen?). But you'll need to find something that you have in common with her, preferably a problem-solving reason.

Take our Angharad. Maybe Buster's had the shits for the last month. You get into a discussion about it, where she moans that she has to do all the picking up of the shit seeing as her fella is away defending the country on a tour of duty with his big, massive gun. The poor dog's got an arsehole like a Japanese flag and the house is beginning to smell like a Biffa bin. You sympathise with her plight and then later on that night, you come home and Google 'dog diarrhoea'. Next day, you happen to be talking to her and you mention that your nan's recommended introducing kibble to Buster's diet, which should add some solidity to her dog's stools. She'll ask where she can get this so-called kibble and you can then ask her if she's on Facebook and you can send her the details.

Add her as a friend and carry on chatting there as you would have done in work (after you've been through her entire photo collection first – head to past holiday pictures of when she went to Majorca if you're after some nice bikini pics).

5. FROM FRIENDSHIP TO FLIRTING

Once you're on Facebook, that's when the fun can really begin. She's accepted you into her (online) life. It's a big step towards you slipping her the truncheon of love.

Subtle flirting by 'liking' some of her more risqué pictures – like the one of her eating a banana. Be careful not to go 'liking' all of the ones with her in a bikini or dressed up as St. Trinians - it'll pop up over all your friends' news feeds and her fella will soon catch onto the fact that you want her stoat.

Inbox her every now and then about day-to-day stuff but don't harass her. If she doesn't reply, she may be busy (other people have lives to be getting on with). Be patient. If she changes her profile picture, inbox her saying how lovely it is but don't try getting involved with flirty or smutty remarks. Remember what I told you about how you make her **feel**? She's invited you into her online world - respect it and don't make yourself too at home too soon. You're not there yet- you're just building up a head of steam.

Try and stay away from getting involved with 'comment conversations' if it involves her boyfriend, husband or family, especially if you haven't been Facebook friends with Angharad that long. She'll get questions like 'Who's this arsehole liking everything you write or comment on?' from her fella. Remember those arms that can move mountains and that gun that could probably take out a tank? They could soon be breaking your neck.

Before long, when you feel that you've got a good friendship going, you can start turning every day conversations to flirty ones. This is a critical part of the seduction process as it means you're now moving into the right area of the park to make your move.

Start by tentatively mentioning things to do with sex. Don't link you and her to it on your first attempt - it could be something as simple as:

'Oh. Did you see that story in this week's Bella magazine about the woman who orgasms every time she farts?' or something of that ilk (better examples available on request).

Angharad's immediate response will give you some indication of how she views sex. If she replies with something like:

'No. I don't read that shit. What time are you in work tomorrow? I need those the phone number of that pet shop that sells that kibble', it's likely that your quarry is not particularly interested in indoor athletics, especially with you. You may wish to consider implementing your Exit Strategy if she doesn't bite on your second attempt. She may think that you look far too much like Russell Grant or someone similar.

If, on the other hand, her reply is something along the lines of:

'Fuck yes! If that was me, I'd be eating baked beans and boiled cabbage for breakfast every day!', you can likely assume that she enjoys that kind of thing. This is a good sign if you are looking to seduce her.

Feel free to develop your conversations about sex at this juncture. Don't ask too many personal questions if you get the feeling that she's uncomfortable. There's a difference between casually mentioning an article in a Bella magazine and asking her outright whether she likes a good fisting during Emmerdale.

By now, you should get the feeling as to whether the seduction process is going well or not. If all's going well, you're doing mighty fine and I congratulate you on your work so far. You've learnt well. If not, again, consider using your Exit Strategy.

If you're on the more successful road, things should move along fairly swiftly. You'll be dropping hints that you find her highly attractive and that she turns you on. She'll be thrilled that she feels so irresistible and hopefully, this will start getting things moving downstairs for her. This is what you are aiming for at this point - getting her moist in Knickersville. You'll be wanting to get her moist on a fairly regular basis.

Sending Your First Cock Picture

This is a monumental step towards your goal. It's a bit like Neil Armstrong stepping onto the Moon or Alan Bradley getting run over by a Blackpool tram. Sort of.

You're going to want your third leg to look as inviting as a fry-up breakfast the morning after the night before. You'll want it to look solid, masterful and long enough to tickle her uterus with. Ideally, you'll want it to look as if she can hang a wet donkey jacket on it. And despite the old adage that 'size isn't everything', size IS everything. You'll be wanting to be known as 'The Walking Tripod'. You can't go satisfying any woman with just a two-inch acorn. And even if you do own a two-inch acorn, you'd at least like to have a go trying. The trick is to make your love truncheon look a little bit bigger than it is in real life. But not too much. Don't be tempted to use a picture of a mammoth one off the internet because if and when you do get Angharad to bed, she's going to be pretty disappointed to say the least. You could be sent packing before you've even got to 'feed her horse'. If you're not particularly well-endowed, try shaving your 'Sherwood Forest', thus gaining you an extra inch or so.

Try experimenting with angles and lighting. A picture of a penis free-floating in space won't give any indication of exactly how big your tool is – you need to give it some sort of perspective at least. For those of you who were at the back of the queue when decent wangers were being handed out, try filling your entire photo with your 'bookie's pencil'. By taking a photo this way, you can go from an 'Argos biro' to 'Godzilla attacking Tokyo' with one snap of your camera.

Magic.

Angharad will feel a hot throb of a thrill when she sees it.

If you are pretty happy with the size of your beast, don't be tempted to go holding it up to a ruler or a marrow just to give it perspective. That's just a bit too cheesy and she'll think that you're a big head. Just 'accidentally' have something in the background to give it some scale.

Never use a flash when taking a picture of your old boy. Never, never, never. Not in a million years. Why not? Well…just go ahead and try it. I guarantee that it'll look like some lilly-white deep-sea creature photographed in the depths of the Loch Ness. Maybe try opening your curtains just a touch to let some natural light in but be careful that the nosy old fella from down the road isn't passing your house just as you try getting the perfect picture.

Taking a photo from down between your legs can sometimes make things look more impressive in my experience. If you don't have extra long arms, get your nan to take a few shots. If you've got small hands, try holding your todger to make it look bigger in comparison. Jeremy Beadle used to use that old trick apparently.

Don't be tempted to take any 'in the mirror' shots. It's likely that you'll be concentrating so hard on getting the right shot that you'll omit to remove your skid-marked Y-fronts from the background.

Keep your face out of the frame too. As we'll learn later, should you need to revert to your Exit Strategy, if your face is an incriminating photo, you're doomed. No amount of attempting to convince people of Photoshopping trickery and that it's all a big set up just won't wash. Aside from that, lads can't really do 'sexy' faces. Girls can of course. But we either end up looking like we're confused or sniffing for a gas leak.

Talking Dirty

Assuming that your cock picture was well-received (and/or she sent pictures back), you'll be at a stage where you can start talking dirty. Dirty talk (or sexy talk, naughty talk etc) involves using language and imagination to drive your quarry into a wild sense of lust for you. If she's willing, you can even do this verbally over the phone but in most instances, this can be done via text, email or Facebook.

Back in the olden days, none of this was really possible of course. The unstoppable march of technology has really aided the seduction process for the modern man. The aim of your dirty talk is to stimulate your girl's major senses: sound, sight and touch. It'll increase her desire for you and the more you do it, the more the sexual tension will ramp up - paving the way for you to suggest what you've been aiming for all along - the shag.

If you are texting, be careful if you have your predictive text on. 'I want to lick your pussy' can easily be sent as 'I want to kick your puppy'. Buster won't be too happy with this and for you and Angharad, it'll be a real passion-killer.

Drop a hint that you're willing to make it happen for real - get the idea into her head. If she still hasn't slapped you across the face, you could be well on your way to that ultimate goal that we were talking about earlier on. Don't pressurise her though. If you've done a good enough job of creating that desire, she'll decide where and when to meet.

It may happen unexpectedly. I had one particular experience with one girl in a previous job where myself and a girl (we'll call her Lucy) decided to meet in a downstairs toilet on a floor that was unused.

But if you're looking to do things properly, you may want to offer Angharad an open invite to your apartment. Tell her that the view from your balcony extends over Cardiff Bay. Tell her that your apartment is carpeted throughout with heavy-pile carpet. Tell her that you'll give her a spare key to your apartment, and that on one particular night, you'll be waiting for her in your bath. All she has to do is decide whether she want to come over.

And whether she wants to let herself in…

6. ENDGAME

So this is what it's all been leading up to - that moment when you can finally complete your seduction and move onto someone else.

But first – Angharad.

Depending on how well your seduction process has gone, it's up to you whether you want to do the whole take-her-out-for-dinner-and-then-come-back-for-some-choreplay or whether you want to just get straight at it.

If you've offered her the spare key to your apartment, tell her to let herself in - you'll be in the bath waiting for her. Tell her to wear nothing but her underwear and a long coat.

Maybe she'll compliment you on your heavy-pile carpet as she comes through the bathroom door to see you sitting in the bath, surrounded by bubbles and candles. You'll return the compliment by telling her how beautiful she looks. It's about how she **feels**. Be confident. Tell her that you knew she'd come over. She'll appreciate your confidence.

She'll act shy, and she may place a finger in her mouth playfully. You'll ask what she's wearing underneath her coat.

She'll slowly drop her long coat to the floor and stand there in front of you in nothing but a matching bra and knicker set and a set of high heels. There will be a slight 'plop' as you 'up periscope' in the bath.

With a flick of your fingers, your Steepletone CD player will start playing the Richard Clayderman CD that you loaded earlier. The beauty of preparation eh?

The edge of her (face) lips will curl as she starts to sway to the easy-listening music. You'll watch entranced, sipping your champagne from your Stella Artois chalice. She'll slip a thumb under her bra strap, pulling it out and away from her body and biting her bottom lip.

You'll tell her what an amazing body she has. It's about how you make her **feel**. Her big bosoms will heave over the top of her boulder holders. You'll be transfixed. Her gaze won't deviate from yours.

She'll step out of her high heels but accidentally step on the orange Bic blade you'd been shaving your bollocks with earlier. Losing her balance, she'll fall to the left, banging her head on the shelf where you keep your collection of Lynx body sprays.

It will break the ice. You'll both laugh it off before she collects herself and carries on stripping, reaching behind and unbuckling her bra. Clutching the cups from the front, she'll then turn away from you before dropping it to your heavy pile carpet, peering over her shoulder to make sure you're watching.

She'll turn to face you again, holding her Mitchell brothers and smiling. Her eyes will wander down your naked body until you feel her brown eyes resting on your Uncle Percy. She'll smile and slowly lick her lips in anticipation. Uncle Percy will stand boldly to attention while she steps forward and then once again, turns away from you.

This time, she'll bend over right in front of you. You'll splutter on your champers. And then, with her two thumbs, she'll slowly pull her knickers down and over her peachy arse.

There in all its glory will be what you've been wanting all along - her throbbing kebab.

Tell her how much you've been thinking about this moment. Tell her to get into the bath.

And before you start thinking of ways to thank me for getting you to this point, just relax and enjoy yourself. Don't mention me by name at this point. You can always leave me some positive feedback on Amazon as a way of thanks when she's gone home.

So you're in the bath together. You're all slippery and shiny like someone's gone and covered you in Trex. And from that moment on, it's pretty much up to you what you do and how you do it.

From the bath, the bedroom is pretty much the next stop on the Voyage of Vulva.

There are some basic dos and donts that you should be aware of however:

• **DO** take your socks off while you're at it. This is no American porn film.

• If she's wearing lingerie, **DON'T** make any comments referring to her looking 'like she's modelling for scatter cushions'. Trust me on this one.

• **DON'T** burp loudly in her face as you go in for your first kiss, especially if you've been on the Limburger Cheese earlier in the day.

• If you're kissing her, **DON'T** overdo it with the tongue. No girl is going to want to feel like she's got a Labrador on her, trying to get a bone out of a hole in her face.

• **DO** try exploring her body before going in for the plunge with the beaver. Try using your tongue and 'growling at her badger'. If she fanny farts in your face, don't make a fuss about it. Simply let the warm winds of love flow through your hair and carry on working at the coalface as if nothing has happened. A woman who is aware that she fanny farts in your face is going to feel absolutely mortified. If this is the case, and if she attempts to apologise or move away, simply tell her how much you love being fanny-farted in the face on. Put her at ease. Tell her just to lie back, relax, and let it all out. Better out than in - that's what they say. It's about how you make her **feel**.

• For your own safety, **DO** make sure that she is moist enough before trying to push the old boy in there. Early pushing can result in the snapping of your 'banjo string'. That's the little stringy bit underneath and at the helmet end of your thunder rod. Snapping this will result in the bedroom looking like a murder scene in one swift thrust. Your GP will also go into an adjoining room for a good old laugh when you visit him the following day. They may even call in medical students to come and have a look (and a snigger).

• If you're in the cowboy position (you on your back and she's riding you like Tonto would), **DON'T** attempt to play Buckaroo. This is where you call out the name of a former lover very loudly and then attempt to hold her on as she tries to wriggle away and dismount. This can result in serious facial injuries, especially if your Stella Artois chalice is within reach of your woman.

• On **NO** occasion, ask her 'Who's the Daddy?' If she's not on the pill, you could be answering your own question.

• If you're going to talk during sex, **DON'T** mention your plans for a fresh layer of artex to be added to the ceiling or that the room could do with a new fitted wardrobe from B&Q.

• If you're going to 'blast off' in her face, **DO** have the common decency to pre-warn her about it. Never assume that she's going to 'take it like a bitch'.

• **DON'T** make your cum face look like you're gunning for first place in the World Gurning Championship. If she places a horse collar over your head at any point during your ejaculation, you know that you should be at this year's Egremont Crab Fair instead.

• If you still haven't offered her a drink by this point, **DO** tell her that you're sorry and that you'll buy her a chicken soup in work tomorrow from the vending machine.

• Only insert a courgette into her **IF** she is consensual with it. She may not want to get into vegetable sex within the first ten minutes.

• **DON'T** go fantasising about Angharad's best friend Tracey being there with you. You're trying to make Angharad feel like she's a million dollars, remember?

After you're happy with your performance and you really can't go at it any more (a man's worst request – 'again'), a woman will feel like cuddling, or as we call it here in Wales, cwtching (pronounced 'cutching' or 'cooching').

While this is all very boring and dull for you, giving your seductee a cwtch will ensure that she's not sent home in a taxi feeling like you've just used her. Try and judge it so that it's not too short. Don't go looking at the bedside clock every minute. Take your time. She'll feel that you do at least, have some feelings for her and that you've shared something special together, even if it was illicit.

7. AFTERGLOW

Congratulations my friend.

She's headed home and you can now relax. You've now successfully seduced the woman you were wanting to pork. Sit back, crack open an ice cold beer and give yourself a big old pat on the back. Reminisce about bending her over the edge of your bath. Bask in the afterglow a while. Savour every carnal second. You've earned it. Well done my friend.

Why You Should Never Gloat About It To Your Work Colleagues.

So you walk into the office with your head held high on the morning after. You haven't washed so that you can still occasionally get the waft of her perfume and her sex. You've decided what you wanted and damn you, you went out and got it.

You take your seat at your desk and peer into the computer screen. You can't help but notice a wide smile beaming right back at you in the screen's reflection.

Your heart bulges and flutters as SHE struts into the office and takes her seat. You gaze over to her over your strong morning coffee and think to yourself 'Only 12 hours ago, I was inside her'. You catch her eye and you exchange knowing smiles. She blushes, pushing her hair back behind her ear and sitting at her desk.

What next?

More seduction? More good times?

Actually no.

Sorry?
I said no.
Not straight away anyway.
First you need to deal with the pay-off.
Yes.
The pay-off.

You didn't really think that you could have all this fun and not pay for it in some way did you?

You go out and get drunk, you have a hangover the next day. You smoke twenty cigarettes a day and then find out that you're dying of lung cancer. It's called a pay-off.

Where there is an action, so too is there a reaction. I think Einstein waffled on about it in is Law Of Relativity. Probably. Actually, probably not. I don't really know what I'm talking about to be honest. But it is the law.

What did I tell you at the very, very beginning? Go back. Go on. I'll meet you back here. That's right.

Trust no-one. Not even me.

And certainly not your best mate at work, Terry.

Terry takes his seat next to you and turns on his computer. Further up the office, Angharad stands and bends right over her desk, trying to figure out why her monitor won't fire up.

Terry turns to you, his lips pursed and says: "Aw mate. I'd ruin her."

You just can't stop yourself.

"I already have mate. Last night. She was awesome."

As soon as you utter those words, you are

doomed. From this moment on, it's all downhill.

"Fuck off you did." Terry will retort.

"No I did. Honest. I've got the photos to prove it."

Terry won't believe a word of it.

"I'll believe it when I see them." Terry will say.

"Promise not to tell anyone?"

"Yeah course."

You'll take your phone from your pocket and swipe the screen. Your chest will throb with the excitement of showing off your conquest. Flicking through your photos, Terry's jaw will drop. Admitting defeat, he will stand and offer you a hand.

"Mate. I salute you." he will say.

You'll probably find that you spend the rest of the day feeling like a real stud. Angharad may walk past the desk and give you a knowing glance. Terry will notice this unspoken exchange and lean far back in his office seat, finger and thumb on chin and giving you the International Sign of the Blow Job.

But you'll head home that night feeling a little uneasy. Why? Well because you've told Terry. And Terry's a bit of a twat. The reason you wanted him to know that you'd tromboned Angharad was precisely because of that reason. You wanted to show Terry who the real stud of the office was. Not him. Not Terry the Twat. But you've got this horrible feeling in the pit of your stomach. Like something's going to spectacularly backfire.

Later that evening, just as you're at home, in front of the telly, after you've polished off a pizza and a few beers to congratulate yourself, you'll get a text. It'll be from Angharad. Your heart will race again. You'll quickly clamber over to the other side of your leather settee to pick up your phone.

Another picture? More dirty talk? A request to pop over and replay last night's filth in graphic, pornographic detail perhaps?

Erm. No.

The first thing you'll notice about the text is that she's shouting. How do we know this? Well, she's written it all in capitals. This is not a good sign.

The next thing you'll notice is that every drop of blood in your body will drop to your feet as you begin to read your text message. You'll go hot and cold at the same time. Your entire body will fizz right to the top of your head like a big old glass of freshly-poured lemonade.

The message will read something similar to this:

"WHAT THE FUCK DO YOU THINK YOU'RE PLAYING AT? I'VE JUST HAD TERRY AND HIS MATES FACEBOOKING ME ASKING IF THEY COULD COME OVER AND JIZZ ON MY FACE."

You'll receive several dozen similar texts, asking you to explain your reasons for telling Terry about your night of pleasure and calling you all the names under the sun. Her language will be colourful, fruity and certainly not in keeping with the business-like persona she gives off at work.

You'll consider lots of things over the next half hour or so – ranging from whether to reply to her texts (not that you'll get a chance as they'll be piling in at a rate of three a minute) through to wondering if your passport is still in date and what it's like to live in Canada.

You'll eventually decide to ignore her texts

but you won't be able to sleep that night. You'll lie in a darkened room, facing the ceiling which will keep lighting up with blue light from your phone. This is likely to last a few hours before you'll eventually turn your phone off in despair.

Every possible scenario will run through your head. Who else has Terry told? What if her fiancé finds out? He's a marine commando. Surely he will track you down with his night-vision goggles and shoot you in the head with his big gun? Maybe he's trained in the art of torture? You've seen it in the films haven't you? The thumbscrews, the hot pokers and those big electrical things they stick on your bollocks?

But before you get start carried away with packing a suitcase and booking a flight to Vancouver, it's worth understanding the female psyche.

Let's look at what makes women so angry.

8. WHAT MAKES WOMEN SO ANGRY?

Pricks like you.

9. WHAT HAPPENS NEXT?

Why Your Exit Strategy is a Load of Hairy Old Bollocks

Now that we know the reason why women get so angry, let's look at why the Exit Strategy you worked on earlier is a load of bollocks.

Once you're in a situation like this, there is no going back. Once you've turned that friendship into flirting (see Chapter Five), your life is doomed. It's like jumping off a cliff – once you've committed to the jump, and to shifting your weight from the cliff edge to the void – that's it. There's no way back – even if you do change your mind half way down. Think back to all those cock pictures you sent. The ones with your face in like I told you not to send. You think she deleted them all? Oh she told you that she had, did she? And you believed her?

What about all those dirty emails you sent to each other in work? Remember the ones you wrote about wanting to bend her over your desk and 'giving it to her large'? Oh, you deleted it did you? Very smart. You didn't think that IT backed up every email? You didn't realise that their boffins can read any email you've sent – even the ones you've deleted?

What about all those dirty conversations you had on Facebook? Can you be totally sure that all of them were in fact conversations with Angharad herself and not her psycho beefcake of a fella? After all, they share the same passwords for their accounts. They're a couple and they share everything. Her password is also written down on a yellow sticky note that's stuck to the lid of her laptop. You did know that didn't you? No. You didn't. And as for that communication ninja analogy I mentioned – yeah, that's a load of old bollocks too.

So. Whatever you've planned in your Exit Strategy, it's likely to be as useless as tits on a fish. You cannot explain away anything. So where do you go from here?

Facebook Smear Campaigns

Having used Facebook as a powerful weapon of choice in your seduction mission, you may find that it's now turned and aimed squarely at you.

In the right hands, like Angharad's, Facebook is capable of bringing down an entire country, never mind an insignificant individual like yourself. You've every right to be afraid.

The first thing you'll notice as you turn your phone on and log in to Facebook, is that you'll be deleted as a Facebook friend from your former seductee. Whilst this is hurtful at first, worse will follow when she actively blocks you, rendering you unable to see what she's posting about you. Whatever you think she's posting, in reality, it'll be 100 times worse.

Now remember that photo you took of your penis, accompanied with the words 'I've called my cock 'The Truth' because most women can't handle 'The Truth'' – do you remember it? You may find that it will have already done the rounds on Facebook while you were sleeping overnight.

The first you'll really know about anything will be when people start sniggering at you in the office the following day. As you breeze into the office, whispers of 'Acorn Dick' and other such names can possibly be banded around. Don't blame me – I did advise you on using the correct lighting and angles.

You may feel slightly paranoid that people are talking about you. Just because you're feeling paranoid, doesn't mean that they are talking about you. But in this instance - yes they are.

It's also quite possible that when you arrive at your desk, you may find the teddy that you bought Angharad is sat forlornly in front of your monitor. It won't look quite the same as it did when you bought it for her - not without a head and being impaled with pins all over him. The pen stuck up his arse will likely be one of yours.

Terry will arrive with his customary brashness albeit with the slight whiff of stale hangover. Try not to twat him too hard, as he may fall backwards onto his desk, catching his head on his stapler on his way to the floor. This will cause a bit of a scene that you could really do without at this stage.

You'll find the First Aid kit in the stationary cupboard to help with his split lip.

How to Block Punches

An awkward situation could arise when you get up to grab a coffee from the vending machine later than morning.

This situation would involve you meeting Angharad by the vending machine as she too, decides that it's time for a hot drink. Whatever you do, don't attempt to talk about Quavers getting stuck in the machine. You're way past that, my friend. She may look visibly angry and upset, as this would be the first time that she's been able to get hold of you and express her anger at telling Terry.

Remember - it's how you make her **feel**.

Should she try to punch you hard in the face, I found that a blocking technique would have been preferable to screaming like a big girl. A block is called a 'parry'. Boxers do it, but the move goes a long way back in martial arts. Any sort of striking art will teach you how to deflect punches.

A good parry involves very little movement; otherwise your hands move too much and it opens up your defence. Against a right-handed woman throwing a straight jab at you with her left, your left hand will make a tiny slap to the right as you step to the left with your front foot. Ideally the punch will just miss your face. You may catch sight of her expensive diamond engagement ring as it whistles alarmingly close to your face.

Should you pull off this block successfully, she could find herself off-balance and may topple forward slightly. This is the perfect time for you to make a run for it in the relative safety of the open-plan office.

However, she may come running after you at this point, screaming like a banshee. If this does occur, you're probably best off running back out to the vending machine and pretending that none of this is happening. Not that it'll help of course.

How To Face a Employment Disciplinary Meeting

Before long, every one of your so-called friends will start to desert you. They'll all start taking sides with seductee (also now known as 'The Victim') and you'll become known as the 'Dirty Pervert' and 'The Family Breaker-Upper'. After Angharad takes time off sick to 'get over her issues' (yeah - what's the matter with her?), you may also be called in to answer questions about your professional conduct at work.

You'll receive a letter from Head of HR which will read something along these lines:

'Dear Mr Evans,

Following a formal complaint from Angharad *******, you are invited to attend a hearing at Bissman House on Wednesday 24th at 4pm where the following issues will be discussed:

• Inappropriate use of Bissman communication systems, in particular the mis-use of Bissman email systems.

• Gross violation of ethical standards on company premises and in company time.

• A gross breach of trust from someone in a managerial position.

Further to previous meetings where a final warning was issued, I am obliged to inform you that the Company has now reached the point where it is considering dismissing you. This hearing is your opportunity to formally respond to these issues.

The meeting will be conducted by Clare Burch and Hannah McGovern. You are entitled, if you wish, to be accompanied at the hearing by a work colleague or a trade union representative. Please advise me by Tuesday 23rd 5pm if you wish to exercise this right.

Yours sincerely.
Clare Burch'

At this point, you'll soon find out who your real friends are and it's likely that you'll realise that this figure comes in at a big fat zero. It's likely that you'll be heading into your meeting on your own so it's a good idea to type up some sort of defence that you can refer to during the meeting. Half a side of A4 should do it, if that.

The meeting will probably take place in a small, sweaty room and you'll feel very much a criminal. In many ways, you are. The charges will be read out to you and you'll refer to your half sheet of A4 and soon realise that you may as well wipe your arse with it. The meeting won't last too long and you'll be asked to leave your ID badge and keys to the company's white BMW 6 Series with security as you leave.

Yes, they really can do that. And yes, it's as easy as that. Darren the security guard is likely to dig the knife in further as you hand him your ID card and car keys by mentioning something about 'that must have been one hell of a shag to have a pay-off like this'. Even Darren knows about pay-offs.

All eyes WILL be on you as you clear your desk (don't pretend that you don't care). Don't forget to take the decapitated teddy with you as you leave – he'll still be sat there with pins sticking out of all parts of his body.

As you no longer have your executive company car, Cardiff Bus offers a regular and straightforward bus service to the Bay, back to your apartment. Current fare is £1.80 for a single.

On arrival home, you may wish to pack a

small bag and head to your nan's house for some TLC. Hopefully she'll have some Coco Pops in from her recent visit to Iceland. If not, Lau's Chip Bar stays open till 10pm most week nights. They do a nice Clark's pie and a great line in battered fish.

During this stay at your nan's, you may start getting threatening texts from your seductee. She may still be angry or she may have calmed a little. Be careful if she does seem moderately at ease with everything - it could indicate that she's coldly plotting a brutal revenge against you. She may inform you that she's having to tell her soldier boyfriend about everything so that he doesn't have to find it out via a mutual friend.

At this point, your anal nerve may desert you, rather like your friends have. Imodium can be bought in capsule form if you have trouble swallowing normal-shaped tablets.

Turning to drink

Drink can be an effective way to temporarily blank things from your memory, but like most things that feel good at the time, there is a pay-off. Milk Thistle Liquid Extract is a good remedy for a hangover. I recommend dropping 50ml of this taste-free liquid into a glass of water before you go to bed and in the water you drink throughout the next day.

You will find however that keeping up a drinking problem can be an expensive hobby and before long, the last of your wages will have dried up. Your life of living beyond your means will catch up with you and soon it'll be time to clear your rented apartment out and move in with your nan on a permanent basis.

You may regret giving your seductee a spare key to let herself into your apartment too. Thinking ahead like any sensible-thinking woman, she will have kept it. Women can be cruelly creative with their revenge - none more so than sprinkling several boxes of cress seed into your lovely heavy wool-pile carpet, watering it, and then turning the heating on while you spent that time wallowing at your nan's house.

When you finally visit your flat to collect your stuff, you may have trouble opening the door to your apartment due to the sheer amount of cress growing there. There are some good carpet restorers who can be found online but none of them will be able to repair this. Your nan should be able to give you some of her life savings (she may have to dip into her pension too) to help repay the landlord for the damage done to the carpets.

Even after this, drink will appeal to you - it'll make the voicemail you have from your seductee, telling you that she's pregnant seem like it's just a bad dream. In addition, you won't feel the sharp pain of a marine's fist slamming into your face when you happen to bump into him in the Fruit & Veg section of Tesco. Remember to thank the old man for saving you from a further beating over the bags of corguettes. Oh yes - the courgettes - oh the irony of it. You couldn't make it up.

• Hopefully, your nan should come to the rescue when your debtors start turning up on your nan's doorstep and demanding repayments. It'll be a sad state of affairs but with the money she makes from selling the house she's lived in for 70 years, she should be able to cover the cost of living in The Cedars retirement home. And with the little money that's left over, you should just about be able to afford to get yourself a Fiat Panda Dynamique.

• This will be your home for the next 10 months until you can get yourself a job in a call centre, giving out the times of trains and thinking up ways to earn some money by writing a shitty book like this and trying to flog it online.

There will also come a day when you'll pass Bissman House in your Fiat Panda Dynamique. It'll be one of those tall, posh buildings you see down Cardiff Bay, opposite the two-bedroomed executive apartment block with the indoor pool and balconies and views over the Bay where you once ate freshly sliced grapefruit and sipped Hacienda La Esmeralda coffee.

And you'll drive past your old office and look up. And you'll wonder if Angharad is back in work yet, sitting there, still twirling her hair round her Parker pen and still leaving lipstick on her paper coffee cup. She'll probably be wearing a very expensive wedding ring and your seat will be taken by Terry the Twat.

Like I told you at the very start, **trust no one**.

About the Author

Ricardo Del Monte (Richard Evans) still works for the Rail Times Enquiry Service and has recently been promoted to ticket sales.

Published by Honey Farm Books
www.honeyfarmbooks.com

CPSIA information can be obtained
at www.ICGtesting.com
Printed in the USA
LVOW04s0952160117
521098LV00016B/402/P